For Abi
(the other author of this book)
with much love
M.L.

For Peter and Simone
Pippa, Rob and Mia
A.R.

First edition for the United States and Canada published in
2006 by Barron's Educational Series, Inc.

First published in Great Britain in 2006 by
Orchard Books
338 Euston Road
London NW1 3BH

Text copyright © Michael Lawrence, 2006
Illustrations copyright © Arthur Robins, 2006

The right of Michael Lawrence to be identified as the author
and of Arthur Robins to be identified as the illustrator of
this work has been asserted in accordance with
the Copyright, Designs and Patents Act, 1988.

All inquiries should be addressed to:
Barron's Educational Series, Inc.
250 Wireless Boulevard
Hauppauge, NY 11788
http://www.barronseduc.com

Library of Congress Control Number 2005937374

ISBN-13: 978-0-7641-5998-5
ISBN-10: 0-7641-5998-4

Designed by David Mackintosh

Printed in China
9 8 7 6 5 4 3 2 1

BABY
CHRISTMAS

Michael Lawrence

Illustrated by
Arthur Robins

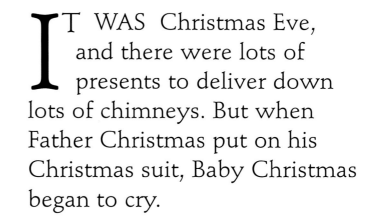

IT WAS Christmas Eve, and there were lots of presents to deliver down lots of chimneys. But when Father Christmas put on his Christmas suit, Baby Christmas began to cry.

"Oh dear," said Mother Christmas.

"Oh dear, oh dear, oh deary-me. What can we do to cheer you up?"

To keep Baby Christmas amused,
Mother Christmas dressed him up in
his Baby Christmas suit and sat him
in his Baby Christmas sleigh.
She even gave him a sack of toys
to pretend to deliver.

"There! Now
you're just like
Father!"

But then . . .

"My Christmas cookies!"
Mother Christmas cried.
And away she went to rescue them
before they burnt to

a frizzle,

a frazzle,

a fruppety-froo.

While Mother Christmas was gone another nose began to twitch.

"Nun-nun-nun-nooooooose!"

said Baby Christmas.

Rudolph Junior's nose had never glowed before, but he knew what it meant.

It meant that he was old enough to fly!

"Ho-ho,"
said Baby Christmas.

"Wa-heee,"
said he,
as out they flew into
the dark and frosty night.

Father Christmas was about to set off when Mother Christmas noticed that Baby Christmas was missing.

And where was Baby Christmas?

Why, flying
around the
world with
Rudolph
Junior!

Lights
twinkled and winked
and winkled
and twinked
from
one end
of the world
to the
other.

"Ooo," said Baby Christmas.

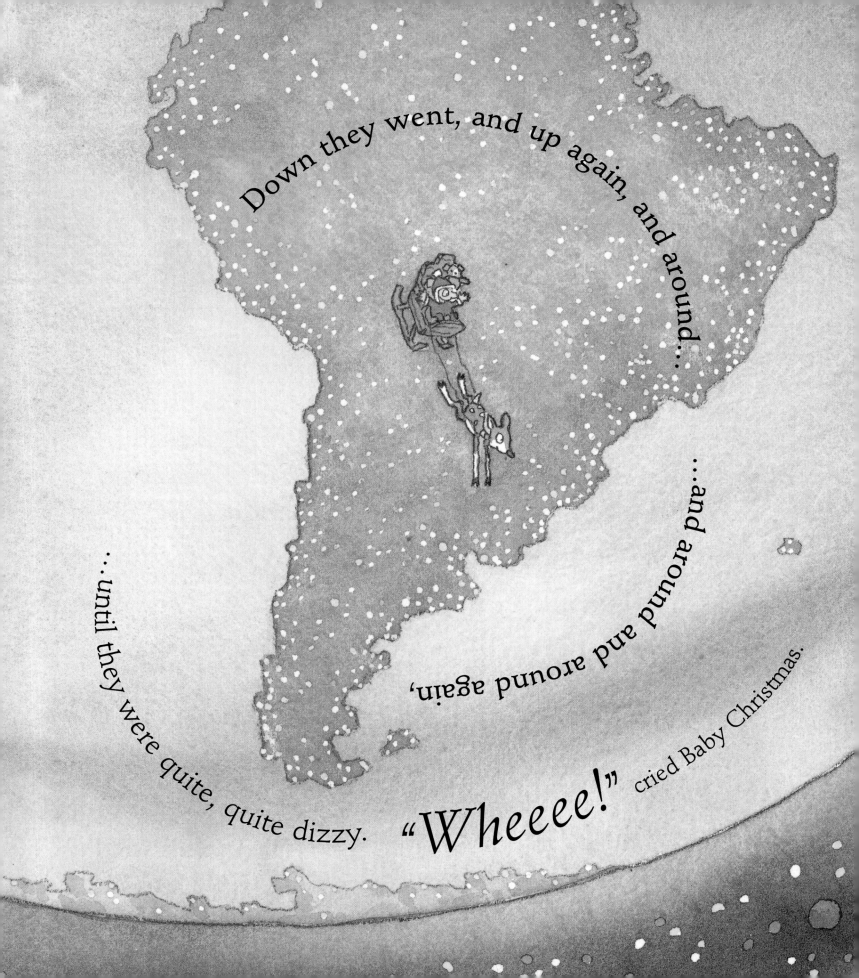

Down they went, and up again, and around...

...and around and around again,

"Wheeee!" cried Baby Christmas.

...until they were quite, quite dizzy.

Rudolph Junior landed on a roof. But his hooves **slipped** and *slithered* and **skidded** and *skaddled,* and...

...into the chimney went Baby Christmas!

Down through the tumbly dark, he fell.

Down and down

and down

and down

until...

"Wup!" said Baby Christmas, kerplunking into the hearth.

Mother and
Father Christmas had
searched and searched and
searched for Baby Christmas.

"I want my
bay-hay-hay-
haaay-bee!"

Mother Christmas wailed.

Father Christmas patted her hand.

"Don't fret, Mother. We'll find him. He'll be out delivering presents, you mark my word. A real chip off the old block, that boy."

In the house, far below,
Baby Christmas stared at
the big bright tree,

with its lights…

…and tinsel

…and
silver bells.

Then he
remembered
what Father
did.

"Yappy Kissmus," said Baby Christmas.

Baby Christmas looked
out of the window.

The snow was
so thick out there.

Baby Christmas loved the snow!

Suddenly Rudolph Senior
spied a small red glow,
far, far below.

He'd know that nose
anywhere!

Mother and Father
Christmas ran around
and around in the snow,
as flustered as custard,
as puffed as pastry.

No sign of Baby Christmas!

But **now** they saw him!
And what a fuss they made
over him. They picked him
up and hugged him tight,
and smothered him with
Christmas kisses.

But Father had to get to work. It was the busiest night of the year.
        All those presents to deliver, and he hadn't even begun!

Up,
they climbed,
and up
and up
and up,
into the
dark and
frosty sky.

But as they were nearing home,
Rudolph Junior sneezed.

Aaa–
aaaa–
chooooo!

And when he sneezed he lost his balance.

And when he lost his balance…

...his bright red nose took him in another direction entirely.

After the little sleigh went Mother and Father Christmas. And as they went, a single sound rang out in the dark and frosty night.

A bubbly little sound.

A very Christmassy little sound.

A tinselly little sound.

Baby Christmas laughing!